DOUBLE THOSE WHEELS

NANCY RAINES DAY

ILLUSTRATED BY STEVE HASKAMP

DUTTON C........ NEW YORK

Text copyright © 2003 by Nancy Raines Day
Illustrations copyright © 2003 by Steve Haskamp
All rights reserved.

CIP Data is available.

Published in the United States 2003
by Dutton Children's Books.
a division of Penguin Putnam Books for Young Readers
345 Hudson Street, New York, New York 10014
www.penguinputnam.com

Designed by Irene Vandervoort
Manufactured in China
First Edition
1 3 5 7 9 10 8 6 4 2
ISBN 0-525-46853-6

FOR MY SON, JESSE,
FORMER CAR-CARRIER CONNOISSEUR
AND MATHEMAGICIAN
—N.R.D.

FOR LITTLE LEVI
—S.H.

1

ONE LONE WHEEL

COMES WOBBLING

THROUGH.

DOUBLE THAT WHEEL,

AND YOU'VE GOT...

2
TWO!

PANT, PANT. PUFF, PUFF.

WHAT A CHORE!

DOUBLE THOSE WHEELS

AND YOU'VE GOT...

4
FOUR!

CHUG, CHUG. PUTT, PUTT.

CAN'T BE LATE!

DOUBLE THOSE WHEELS

AND YOU'VE GOT...

DOUBLE THOSE WHEELS—

COUNT THIRTY-TWO!

32

FLASH, FLASH. DING, DING!

ONE STOP MORE.

CLICK, CLACK. WHOO-HOO!
SCREE-EECH. UH-OH!

NO MORE WHEELS.

UP WE GO!

HAPPY BIRTHDAY!

PIZZA'S HERE,
ON THE DOT.

PARTY TIME NOW—

IT'S GOOD AND HOT!